Signed Books and more
www.mattshawpublications.co.uk

Serial Killers

A Collection of Psychological Horrors

Matt Shaw

- Contents -

POV

i.

I had been watching her all evening. It was hard not to really, given how beautiful she looked in the tight, black dress she was wearing. At a guess I would say she was a size ten. At a push, a twelve. Her curves are in all the right places and she truly is mesmerising to watch, as she dances to the club's soulful music.

I would offer her a drink but she's getting enough attention already from would-be admirers. I cannot blame them for chancing their luck. If things were different, or if I was like them, I possibly would have given it a try myself. As it stands though, there is very little point in even giving her a passing *hello*. This doesn't mean I will be going home without her though. My lack of a more conventional approach has never stopped me going home with them before. If anything, my way is easier. It is guaranteed. It takes all the risk of rejection out of the ugly equation.

The object of this evening's desire is standing at the cloakroom window. I watched as she handed a ticket over, a beautiful smile on her so pretty face. Those lips. Those lips so perfectly painted red. I couldn't help but to lick my own lips as I imagined kissing her.

My heart skipped a beat at the thought and a rush of adrenaline surged through me for a pleasant moment as I told myself, we will be kissing before the night is out.

The tired looking idiot behind the counter passed over her long black coat. She draped it over her bare arm and thanked him. A moment later and she was heading towards the club's exit unaware that I was her shadow.

I was pleased to see her heading out alone. So many times, prior to tonight, someone had caught my eye and then left with another person. Sometimes a friend, sometimes a person they'd only just met a few hours earlier. On those occasions I never followed. I just let them go. It was safer that way. Easier to forget about them and move on then get caught and spend however long in prison. Although the number of times I have done this now, I am only delaying the inevitable. Still, I don't exactly want to rush off to prison. I want to get as much enjoyment as I can before I am caught. I want as many nights, like this, that I can squeeze in before the police find me.

ii.

I follow behind at a safe distance, just as I had when she left the club and walked to her car. I catch up with her at the traffic lights but - the moment they turn green - I hang back and give her time to put distance between us.

After ten minutes or so we turned into a small cul-de-sac. It's quiet. Peaceful. I smiled. It's perfect. It's much better than the last woman. She lived in an apartment block which made it virtually impossible to continue our fun. Too many potential witnesses and people to call the cops, if either of us happened to make too much noise. Sadly, noise is something I cannot seem to avoid even when I catch them by surprise. There is always a bit of a struggle. Things smash. Screams emitted. Furniture toppled.

The houses here are detached. We can make more noise here and, I can't help but to smile, I am sure we will make some too, in the most enjoyable of ways imaginable.

I stayed at the end of the cul-de-sac, just around the corner from its entrance. Having been on her tail for so long, I'm not sure how she would have reacted had I turned in there with her. Especially as there aren't many houses in there. She probably knows everyone; all her neighbours. Thinking about it, they probably have weekly book groups or whatever is the equivalent now. Ergh. I almost feel nauseous with such thoughts. I couldn't imagine anything worse than sitting around with a bunch of boring housewives, reading *Twilight*. No thank you.

I watched as she parked her car onto a double-sized drive. There is no garage, so I presume she lives alone. Either that or, whoever she lives with, they aren't home yet - given the empty space. Fingers crossed she lives alone, or they stay out for a few more hours at least.

I pulled the car up against the curbside and watched from afar as she climbed out of her car. I smiled to myself as I tried to figure out why she parked in the space furthest from her house. Had that been me, I would always park as close as possible but then, maybe that's why my step-count is never as it could be.

I shrugged.

A few more minutes to let her get in and then, I'll go a-knocking. I'm genuinely excited. These are the nights I live for. The rest of my evenings are so… dull.

iii.

I knock on the door first. I wait for them to open. When they do, I tell them I have broken down. I tell them they are the only ones who answered their door and I ask to borrow their phone. They usually ask if I don't have a mobile phone to which I tell them, it's out of battery power. Sometimes they let me in. Sometimes they tell me to leave. If they let me in, all good. If I have to leave then - it's all about whether they have access to the property via a window, or something. In the case of apartments, unless they live on the ground floor, it is usually game over at that point. I never force my way through the front door. I am no good at picking locks and the damage would be too obvious if I used something to break it down. Neighbours don't tend to turn a blind eye when they see a smashed door.

I approached the front door. It's red and I find myself humming *The Rolling Stones*. I still don't understand the song, even after all these years. For the record, I don't think a black door would be nice. I think it would be somewhat morbid but, each to their own.

When I was a few feet, a security light came on and my heart immediately skipped a beat. I cast a glance over my shoulder, back towards the other houses nearby. I scanned the area to see if anyone was there. If a neighbour was at a window or taking the trash out - if they saw me then I would be busted before I even started. I would have to retreat.

As luck would have it, the streets are quiet. From behind me, the red door opened, and the pretty lady spoke, 'Can I help you?'

I turned.

'Sorry…' I slipped into my well-versed sales patter, 'My car broke down and I was hoping I could borrow your phone?' A slight pause before, 'I tried your neighbours but, you're the only one who answered…'

'I'm sorry, I'm just about to have my dinner…'

'I just need to call a recovery service. It won't take but a minute…'

She huffed. 'It's late…'

'And I really want to get home.' I added, 'I'll be quick. I'm really sorry about this…'

I could see it on her face that she really didn't want to let me in. I can't say I blame her. I'm not sure how I would react if the tables were turned but then, I've watched a lot of horror movies in my time. I know how these scenarios usually go.

I told her, 'I just need to call them and then I'll go back to my car and wait. Please…'

'Okay. Be quick,' she said with some reluctance in her tone.

'Thank you,' I told her, 'You're a life-saver.'

She stepped back from the door and let me in. I didn't hesitate. The longer I stayed on the doorstep, the more chance there was of someone else spotting us together.

iv.

'There you go,' she said as she pointed me to her home phone. The phone was sitting in a white cradle, upon a small table in the hallway with a telephone directory. I almost laughed when I saw the telephone book. I wasn't aware people still even had those. I thought they more or less died a death when the Internet came about. Why look up a telephone number in a large book when you can just Google it? Still, it is a big and heavy book so will come in handy right about now.

I approached the book and picked it up. 'I didn't know you could still get these,' I said. She said nothing. She just watched me from a few feet away as I started flicking through it. 'Just as well really. Don't know the number of the recovery people off the top of my head,' I said. That was my excuse for picking up the book.

I can see her expression out of the corner of my eye. She genuinely looks pissed off with me for being in her house. Fair enough she might be wanting her dinner - even if it is a bit late - or have plans but, Jesus, she thinks I am stuck out there, with no way of getting help. You would think she would be happy to help me.

'Shit,' I said.

'What is it?'

'I can't even remember how to use these books.' I fake-laughed. 'Google is much easier.'

She sighed and said, 'Here, let me.' She wasn't being helpful for any reason other than the fact she wanted me out of her home faster. But, you know, that was perfectly fine with me as it made her take a step towards me.

As she took her second step, closing the gap between us, I quickly slammed the book shut and swung it hard and fast to her face. As planned, the blow landed with an almighty "crack" which knocked her onto her arse. Before she had a chance to compose herself, I lifted the book up high and brought it down - to the top of her head - hard. She slumped back flat on the floor. This time she made no attempt to get back up. She just made a strange groaning noise from the back of her throat. With no more use of the telephone directory, I dropped the heavy book to the floor too.

v.

'Wake up,' I told her.

'…'

'I said, wake up…'

'… Where… am… I?'

She was dazed and confused. That wasn't unexpected. They always woke up in a similar state if I had hit them about the head with something heavy. I am never surprised by their confusion; I am just grateful that they woke up. Only once did I hit a woman a little too hard and she never did open her eyes again. It didn't stop me spending the night. No sense wasting all that effort but, still, it is nicer when they're awake to experience it with me. What can I say? I like to share.

She asked again, 'Where am I?'

She really was confused. If she just concentrated a bit more, she would have noticed she was still in her home. I had dragged her through to the living room and stripped her naked. I would have liked to have taken her up to bed, just as I wished I had taken others to bed too, but when they live in a two-storey home it is hard for me to get them up there. I have tried on a few occasions but, each time, it sapped me of my energy and the rest of the evening had been a bust as a result.

I had also taped her hands behind her back with the silver tape I'd taken into the house with me, concealed in my jacket. There was also duct tape around her ankles too, but it wasn't so tight that her legs were forced together. There was still enough of a gap for me to get my hands between her legs. In truth I wish I didn't have to put tape on their ankles but... I learned that - even with their hands tied and the exits blocked - these bitches like to kick at me and, if given the opportunity, try and run. So... There is enough tape to stop any of that nonsense but not so much tape that it ruins all my fun.

'What do you want?' she said as she finally came to her senses.

I smiled at her. 'I want to admire you.'

vi.

I was standing above her. Just as I had removed her clothes, I had removed mine too. The majority of her clothes were tossed to the side whilst mine were folded neatly and placed up on her settee, out of the way. Next to my pile was her underwear. When I get dressed and leave her be, I will be taking those with me as I have done with all other ladies I have visited over the months and years.

She struggled against the tape. I didn't tell her to stop. I liked to watch her struggle. I liked to see her body writhing around as a result. The way her breasts jiggle, the way her breath changes - becoming heavier with the effort she puts in. The way her inner thighs rub together.

'You're so beautiful,' I told her.

'Please, let me go. I won't tell anyone.'

'Ssh.'

I ran my hand across my bare stomach. I was desperate to touch myself as I watched her, but I refrained. The longer I wait, the better the climax.

I knelt down next to her and put one hand around her throat with light enough pressure to allow her to breathe but enough to let her know she needs to stop moving now. She did so. I smiled at her. With my other hand I touched her breast and gave it a firm squeeze. When I had first seen her, I felt sure she had fake tits but, they're real. My smile broadened. I hate fake breasts.

Quietly she said, 'Please don't hurt me.'

I told her to shush again as I slid my hand down her stomach and between her legs, forcing them apart so that I could see her vagina. As my fingers brushed her labia, she made a strange whimpering noise as though fearful about what I was going to do next.

I looked up to her face and noticed she had closed her eyes and turned her head away to the side. Does she think - by doing so - that I am going to go away?

As I gently stroked between her legs, I told her, 'Open your eyes. They're too pretty to keep them closed.' When she didn't do as I so kindly requested, I pushed my hand against her vagina. In the process of doing so, I dug in my nails. I repeated my simple instruction, 'Open your eyes.'

She opened them.

'You have such pretty eyes,' I said when she looked at me. Ignoring the fear - and tears - in them, she had the brightest green eyes I had ever seen on a person before. 'I would love eyes like yours,' I told her. My own eyes were a dull grey in colour. They almost looked as though they were misted with cataracts, even though they weren't. It wasn't just her eyes that I was envious of either. I was envious of how soft her skin was and how firm her body. Even when I was her age I don't recall having such a radiant glow about me and my breasts definitely weren't as firm as hers either. Not then and especially not now. Now they just sag.

vii.

I caught a glimpse of myself in a mirror that she had hanging above the fireplace. I was a state.

I momentarily stood up, leaving her to struggle once more, and gave myself a proper look in the mirror. Usually I avoid my reflection but.. Well, I wasn't expecting her to have a mirror in her living room.

My eyes welled up, taking away the joy from the moment.

I am ugly.

The tragic thing is, this isn't because of my age. I had never been what you would consider to be a pretty woman. I always had some kind of skin complaint. My hair never looked good, even after I came fresh from a hairdressers. My eyes - previously mentioned - never gave off a sparkle that attracted the men who'd be desperate enough to talk to me. My stomach was never as flat as other girls - even pre-teenage years. Even my own mother used to refer to me as the ugly duckling. She was wrong though. I wasn't the ugly duckling because at least that grew into a beautiful swan. I was just... Nothing. Not like the ladies I like to follow.

They have something truly special and unique about them which I never fail to notice. I hate it. It's unfair. Why should they be so fucking perfect when there are people like me?

I turned my attention back to her. I told her, 'Stop fucking moving. You're not going anywhere…'

She said again, 'Please… What are you going to do to me?'

I smiled and made my way to my jacket. It was hanging on the back of the living room door. I reached in and pulled out my kitchen knife. Then, I turned to her and said, 'I'm going to make you ugly.' I told her, 'I'm going to make you like me.' As I closed the gap between us, she screamed out loud.

PUNCTUALITY

Dear Mrs. Peters,

I do not know about you, but punctuality is ever so important to me. I feel as though I am one of the only people who believe this to be of importance anymore though but, by the end of this letter, I am sure - if you didn't before - you too will hold "punctuality" in high regard. If you have a moment, please allow me to explain further.

I am not sure what you do for a living. I will be honest; I do not actually care. I used to work in an office though. It was a high-pressured sales job and I cannot say I enjoyed it. What I liked less though were the rushed breaks, be it mid-morning or afternoon breaks, or my lunch hours. You see, I would always find myself rushing around. My break would come, and I would rush to the coffee shop on the corner because I needed a pick-me-up. True enough there was a coffee pot in the communal staffroom but that was like - I imagine - drinking urine. Not for me, no matter the level of thirst I am suffering.

I would get to the coffee shop in a timely fashion, and I would place my order promptly but the little worker-bees behind the counter never seemed to care that I was on a break and my time was precious. They would move at their own pace, and I would always have to run back to the office. By the time I got there, I could not put my feet up and nor could I enjoy my coffee in a quiet moment. I would have to drink it on the "go". It would be the same story for lunch too.

I never take food in from home. I find it a hassle to go home and prepare it for the next day, or even wake earlier to get it ready first thing in the morning. There are two sandwich shops close to the office. I would try them both - on alternating days - and would always find a queue. Unlike in the coffee shop, the queues at least moved fast but I would still have to stand around for a while. It is frustrating. More so because they have an overly large clock hanging on the wall, close to the counter. I would stand there, waiting my turn, watching the minutes of both my lunch hour and life tick down and there would be nothing I could do about it. Even when they were making my sandwich, I would still be counting down the minutes - second by second. By the time my sandwich came through, I would be conscious of the fact that I would not have much time to eat it, without giving myself indigestion. I would take the food back to my office and I would sit in one of the comfortable armchairs (in the communal area) and I would eat, say, half of the sandwich. The other half, to save indigestion, I would eat on my mid-afternoon break. The mid-afternoon break being the only un-rushed break; the only moment of my day where I could sit back, for fifteen minutes, and rest.

Now I know I am not alone in those examples. It is never just me standing in the queues. It is never just me staring at the clock on the wall, or the watch on my wrist, or even the time on my phone. It is never just me "huffing", "puffing" and tapping my foot whilst wishing for faster service. Imagine if service was speedier, or there were better systems in place for the waiting customers - surely stress levels would go down? With less stress, there would be more time to smile at strangers? More time to wish them a good morning, afternoon or evening? A little thing to make the world a nicer, kinder place. If only for that moment. I am not sure about you but I quite like the sound of that.

I also get frustrated when people, whom I am expecting at a certain time, are not punctual. It bothers me that, if they had been on time, we could have had a better table in a restaurant, or nicer seats on the train or bus. We could have seen all the previews at the cinema? Perhaps seen a trailer for another film we might have wanted to watch together at a later date? Or had they been on time we could have enjoyed some drinks at the bar before being seated? Let us not forget that, with them being late, we also start to worry that they are not coming too. That, in turn, leads to more stress and - I am sure you are aware - more strain on the heart, which we both know is not good.

But then I played coy at the start of this letter for I *do* know about you and I *do* know that, *now*, punctuality is important to you. You are simply another example as to why it is so important to be punctual. What I am about to say, you have undoubtedly thought multiple times over the last two weeks or so. That one niggling voice in the forefront of your mind screaming at you, *If only you had been on time to pick your daughter up from practice.*

Just think, you could have been on time to get to the hall where she played sports. You would have been waiting for her, for when she came out. She would have seen you sitting in the car. She would have said goodbye to her friends as they left the hall together. You would have leaned forward in your car seat and fired the old engine up. She would have said "hello" as she climbed in and sat next to you, closing the door behind her. She would have put her seatbelt on and cranked the car's heating up as you pulled away from the space, maybe asking how her practise session had gone. The two of you would have talked about this and that for the drive home, however long that drive would have been. Then, what? Maybe you would have had a takeaway? Maybe you would have had dinner waiting in the oven? A pleasant evening doing your own thing, or spending time together as a family - watching a film, playing a game, sat in the same room reading? I do not know. I am not entirely sure how the "family thing" works as I have never belonged to a family. Not a real one. Anyway, that is what could have come to pass, had you been punctual but, no, you were late. You were late and we know how that story ended.

You got to the hall. Your daughter was not there waiting, and neither were her friends. You tried to call her, but the call was ignored and just went through to voicemail; a voicemail that you left. A voicemail that we both listened to before I disposed of the phone. I wonder, how many voicemails did you leave on that broken phone in the end? How many calls did you make to that cell? How many of those calls made you late for other appointments which, in turn, had other knock-on effects? I do wonder.

Anyway, I am writing to let you know that I have been spending time with your daughter for these past two weeks. You must be very proud of her. She seems like an intelligent young lady. She has done all that I have asked from her, and she has done so bravely and without argument. To begin with she asked me when I would let her go home but when she learned such a question upset me, she stopped asking. Like I said, an intelligent young lady. If only you had been punctual, who knows where her intelligence could have led her in life.

Oh, and speaking of "punctuality", do you not just hate the Royal Mail postal service these days? You post letters to people, but they never arrive on time. This week alone I have been expecting a few packages and they are already a few days late and that too has a knock-on effect. Are the parcels so late they cannot go out as the gifts they were intended for? Did I manage to find it somewhere else, and get it faster? Or in the case of this letter... Whilst I write, your daughter is alive but - with the reported delays in the postal service at the moment, thanks to Christmas - there is a strong possibility that, when you finally receive and read this letter, she will not be.

A pity.

Anyway, do not feel too bad about how things panned out here. You are not the only person in the world who struggles with being punctual and that is the point of this letter. I wanted you to know that there are many more people like you who will, one day, come to rue the day they were not punctual. You are one of many. I just hope in your case that this letter has driven home, to you, the importance of being punctual for whatever it is we are doing. If you have learned no lesson from this then, really, there is no helping you. You will suffer further in life and, with all that is lost in just this one instance for you, that would be a pity.

Kind Regards,

J.

A DAY IN THE LIFE OF…

The meat is gently simmering away in the pan. The stove is on gas mark two. It takes longer to cook this way but I've found it is just a better way of doing it. Any higher and the meat can go from "raw" to "overdone" in too quick a time and, before you know it, dinner is ruined. Anyway - with regards to the timings - I am in no rush; I am eating alone tonight.

It is a pleasant evening outside. To me anyway. Other people complain about the light drizzle and the bitterness to the chill in the air, even about the low hanging fog but, I don't know why, I like evenings like this. You can just close your front door, put some music on in the background, get the fire roaring in the living room and make everything nice and cosy. In that setting, I find I am able to get my head down and just continue with one of my favourite hobbies; sewing. On days when it is sunny outside, warmth in the air and blue skies - I always feel duty bound to go for a walk in the woods, or something. Maybe people walk down the park; all those happy couples going out for evening strolls or walking their dogs. It is pleasant enough, for sure, but by the time I lay down in my bed, and ready myself for sleep, I always feel as though I have wasted my time. That's not the case of evenings like this and when I am sewing.

Tonight, I plan to finish this dress. I started it over a month ago but was forced to stop when I ran out of materials. Thankfully, before night drew in, I had been able to replenish my stocks so - nothing will stop me now.

I gave the minced meat another stir and added some salt in for a little seasoning, not that the meat really required seasoning. It's not as though it wouldn't taste divine without it but, even so, "seasoning" is just something I have had driven into my head over and over after watching so many cooking programs. *It helps bring out the flavours.* Who am I to argue? These chefs have stars to their names, and I struggle not to burn toast. Whatever. As the meat sizzles away now, one thing is for sure, it smells amazing and - once finished - I will add some mash potatoes to the top of it and make myself my own version of a cottage pie. Added bonus about being alone is that there will be plenty of leftovers too so, I can have the same again tomorrow if I just store it in the fridge and then give it zap in the microwave to warm it through.

Satisfied with how dinner was going and safe in the knowledge I had a few minutes more before I needed to do anything else to it, I returned to my sewing machine and resumed my almost-laughable efforts at making this dress. Whilst I enjoyed trying to sew, it is fair to say my sewing is much like my cooking abilities. Actually, thinking about it, my cooking skills are probably a little bit better. It's a shame that when I was growing up, I didn't pay more attention to my mother. She was great at sewing and she would have had this dress finished in no time. Speaking of the dress: I am making a figure-hugging number. Or rather I hope I am making a "figure hugging" outfit. For all I know, by the time I am done, it will be more like a tent. It's not as though I am following a pattern, or anything. Perhaps, if I had been, things could have been both easier and quicker but, whatever. I like a challenge.

The dress is pale pink in colour with a lining of red. I usually wear blacks and blues in my everyday life so I am not sure why I thought such a colour would look good on me but there you go. Life is all about experimentation, am I right?

I managed to get a few stitches into the design when I realised the music had stopped from the other room. I'm hardly surprised given I was only listening to the local radio station but, even so, I don't want to listen to talking or - as I listened closer - the news. I wouldn't mind if they were talking about something worthwhile on there, but they never are. They run through the bulletins (which is fine) but then they decide to try and break it all down and discuss it further, like they have any kind of true insight into what is going on out there? It's just their opinion and nine times out of ten, their opinions are just complete bullshit. Shut up already and get back to playing the music... But they never do; they just waffle and waffle and waffle. No thank you.

I pushed myself away from the kitchen table and walked through to the living room. I stopped dead in the doorway and my heart immediately skipped a beat and then continued to race. There was a man standing in front of my radio. His hands were bloody, his face also smeared. There was a maniacal look on his face as he turned to look at me. He raised his bloody finger to his lips and said, 'Shush... They're talking about *me*!'

On the radio:

'So how many has he killed now?'

'Honestly I've lost count. All I know is that when they catch him, I hope they string him up by the neck. The amount of pain and misery he has caused this city.'

'True but it doesn't sound like they're any closer to catching this guy…'

'He'll make a mistake one day…'

CRUEL

They say I am cruel. "They" being the media, the police, the members of the public yet to meet me. Not just in this country but overseas too. If you read, or hear, anything about me - they all say the same. I am cold, calculated, cruel. Some go far as to call me "sadistic". Out of those things they've called me, the only thing they're right about is how calculating I am. I am very calculating. The reason being, if I wasn't, I would have already been caught. But cold? I am not cold.

'Night-night, daddy!'

My eldest daughter (8) leaned down and gave me a kiss. I was sitting in the living room armchair with my feet up. The television was on. The News. The studio was discussing me, not that they knew who I was. They were just talking about what I had done. I smiled at my eldest and kissed her back. 'Goodnight, sweetheart.' If I were "cold", I would not have wished her a good night. I would not have kissed her back. I would have stayed sat with eyes glued to screen.

My youngest daughter (6) ran in and jumped into my lap. She gave me a big cuddle and I, in turn, squeezed her back. She always got to stay up as late as her eldest sister on a Saturday. Not only did she think she was being treated like "an adult" but her mother and I hoped it meant she wouldn't wake as early on the Sunday morning. The longer she slept in, the quieter the house. The quieter the house, the longer our own lie-in. 'You off as well, Munchkin? I thought we would stay up and watch a film together?'

She looked at me with excitement in her eyes. 'Really?'

I laughed. 'No.'

'Oh.' The disappointment was obvious. Had I been "cold" I wouldn't have felt a little guilty about getting her hopes up like that but, there was a definite pang of guilt. Nothing that I would lose sleep over, mind you.

'Off to bed you go,' I told her with a kiss.

She climbed off me and ran to - and out of - the living room door. I can't believe how much energy she has given she had been playing in the park for the best part of the afternoon. As she exited, my wife entered.

'And - finally - peace,' she said.

I smiled at her. Had I been "cold", I wouldn't look forward to our evenings together. I would have gone out drinking or made myself busy in my office upstairs. It's not as though I don't have a ton of work I could be getting on with.

My wife made her way to the sofa and slumped down into it. She looked at me with those big brown eyes which had so easily hooked me in when we first met. She said, 'You aren't going to come over and join me?' She patted the sofa next to her. There was just about enough space there for me, with the way she had landed. I got up and went and sat next to her. She immediately cuddled in, and I put my arm around her. Had I been "cold", I wouldn't have done this. I would have left her over there, by herself.

My wife grabbed the controller and changed the television station, unaware that I was watching what they were saying about me. Probably for the best, I was only getting myself worked up with their bullshit. Sometimes I honestly believe they say antagonistic things about me in the hope I'll make a mistake in my efforts to prove them wrong.

I'm not stupid but then, "stupidity" is not something they have ever accused me of.

My wife settled on a channel and snuggled in further.

I warned her, 'Don't forget about the film.'

'I know.'

We had already agreed upon a film to watch together. A romance, of all things. Would I be "cold" and still watch such a film? No. I would have steered my wife to something more violent. A horror, perhaps? As it stood, this romance didn't actually look too bad. It had something for her and something for me.

The film would go on at nine o'clock. By putting it on then, we would have given the kids enough time to fall asleep. That way they don't disturb us whilst we try and get into the film, if they play up. We can watch it in peace and quiet and just enjoy it.

9pm and not a minute sooner, nor later.

It's all about the routine.

My life is all about "routine". Everything I do, every movement and moment. I think it all through, I plan it all in my head and, then, I execute it exactly. Some people might consider this a form of mental illness but it's not. By living in such a way, even down to how many strokes I use to brush my teeth in the morning and evening, I am able to avoid stress. All problems are considered carefully before they have a chance to occur, and I have a back-up plan for if things don't go accordingly. If more people were like this in life, I believe the world would be a better - certainly safer -

place but, alas, most people act on impulse and just learn to live with their idiotic decisions.

When the articles refer to me as "calculating", I take it as a compliment. It means they understand how carefully I stop to think things through. It shows they understand I am not unhinged and acting on impulse. It also shows them they need to be smart to catch me. A man with a plan is always one step ahead. I have plans, I have back-up plans, I have alibis, I have everything I need to avoid their eyes falling upon me. If they *do* happen to look in my direction, it will never be for long. I can do what I do for as long as I want and if I did choose to stop, I even have the perfect way out. Like I said, I have a plan for everything. I *am* calculating.

But "cruel"? I can hazard a guess as to why they call me cruel, but they aren't seeing the bigger picture. They're not stopping to think about everything. They're just seeing what I have done to a person and that's that. They then go and form their ill-conceived opinions of me and then try and ram it down the throats of those who don't really know who I am, or what I am about. They just see me as having plucked the eyes from a person before stamping their heads to mush. Or their heartless (and eyeless) bodies left in a pool of blood, with the heart nowhere to be seen, or the eyeless bodies strung up in trees with heavy ropes around their broken necks…

What does amuse me though is how they try and explain my methods. Most noticeably, the reason as to why I remove the eyes. They think it is because I am too ashamed of my crimes. I pluck the eyes from the victims before I kill them so that I don't have to see how the victims look at me, ahead of their demise. It's funny when you think about it because - how can I be "cold" if I also feel "guilt" or "shame"? That alone makes no sense and just shows how much rubbish these so-called professionals actually spout.

Before we even look at the reason as to why I take their eyes though, look at the "victims". I've killed bank managers who refuse people their necessary loans and overdrafts, effectively forcing them onto the streets.

I've killed people I caught breaking into properties or mouthing off to strangers despite having no reason to. I've taken the lives of pimps who run girls who have been forced to sell sex to strangers.

I've killed tradespeople intent on robbing their customers with shoddy work and high prices.

I've killed from all walks of life but each of these so-called "victims" has something in common. They're all scum. In their own way, they are just pieces of shit who play their part in ruining the lives of others. I take their eyes because they are blind to life, so do not deserve to see the potential beauty on offer, if you look hard enough. They are blind to the pain and misery they cause others. They are blind to the despair they cause and blind to the impact of their own cruelness.

I am the cruel one?

I think not.

I am the kind one.

I am the one doing the rest of us a favour by purging the earth of these monsters. They are the cruel ones, not me. One day, the people hunting me might realise that but, I have my doubts.

Until then, I will keep playing my part.

POPCORN

I have not had popcorn since I used to work in the local cinema in town. Working there, I would have it on every break and whenever I went in to watch one of the staff previews. I guess I just *popcorned* myself out by the time I left. It's not that I no longer liked it, it's just I have had *so much* of it. Jesus, I probably ate more popcorn in those two years of working there than you, or anyone else, would eat in their entire lifetime and, no, that is not an exaggeration. That being said, with hunger drumming that familiar beat in my stomach, I was pleased to see a packet of microwave popcorn in the cupboard. It's convenient, it is quick, it is tasty and - better yet - it is perfect food companion for what I am about to watch.

I removed the box from the cupboard and took out what appeared to be the last of the available packets. It's always weird, to me, seeing popcorn like this - small kernels which need microwaving. At the cinema, on our weekly delivery, we literally had bags and bags and bags of the stuff show up pre-cooked. All we had to do was to count it in and set it to the side (in date order). Then, when we were ready to use it, we used to carry it through to the shop floor and just empty it into the warmers. At the end of the evening, we then spooned it all back into the bag, tied the bag up and cleaned the warmer out. We then finished the bag the following day. Some days we could get through six of those bags in a single shift, such was the popularity of the snack and despite the inflated prices the cinema charged for a tub of it. I don't know why people just didn't buy their own from the shops and take that in with them but, then, maybe they prefer it warm. There is something nice about warm popcorn.

Still, our popcorn is an embarrassment compared to what they serve up in America. One large tub of popcorn with extra butter and I am good to go. It is always a disappointment to have that and then come home to the crap we pass off as cinema popcorn but, there you go. I guess it's cheaper and easier the way we do it. Definitely a pity though. We would probably shift more if we made it the same way. Thinking back, I'll never forget the face of one of my customers once. He was from America and here on vacation. He asked for some popcorn and stated he would like it buttered. I told him that wasn't something we could supply and he just looked at me blankly.

He asked, 'So what *do* you do?'

'Sweet or salt,' I told him.

I can't remember what he opted for but - here, today - sweet is what I have apparently. I can eat both variants. I can even tolerate toffee popcorn, as sold in the packets, but the best we do is when it is mixed. A little salt and a little sweetness. That really is the way forward and I'm sure there is some salt knocking around here that I can add to this, should I feel the need.

A quick scan of the packet instructions and I set the flat bag of popcorn into the microwave and clicked through the various options ahead of pressing "start". I stepped back from the microwave as it lit up and - through the window - the plate (and popcorn) slowly started to turn.

A few seconds passed and the popcorn started to pop. To begin with it was just a pop here and a pop there but it wasn't long before all hell broke loose in that brown bag and the popcorn was popping frantically. Just as the kernels expanded into what we know and recognise as popcorn, so too did the brown bag expand; a mixture of air and being forced wider because of the popcorn.

As the room started to fill with the sweet scent of hot popcorn, my mouth actually filled with saliva and I couldn't help but feel a little pang of excitement. I can't believe I haven't had popcorn in so long! This little bag here will most likely kickstart my addiction to it and I'll be back to eating it daily before I realise it.

I laughed to myself; at least I won't be paying cinema prices this time around. Even with staff discount that shit cost an arm and a leg.

When the popcorn finished its time in the microwave, I removed the packet and looked for a clean bowl to tip the contents into. I never like eating it from the bag because it always feels greasy. With a decent-sized bowl in hand, I tipped the packet out into it and was disappointed to note that it a third of the kernels hadn't yet popped.

It frustrates me when that happens because you follow *their* instructions and *their* timings so you would think that all would pop. As it is, it's like they don't even know their own product!

Ah well, no sense ruining the moment.

It's not like none of them popped and I am sure I have enough to eat. Anyway, it might not be their fault. It could well be the microwave is just a piece of shit. It's a different brand to the one I have at home and - in fairness - looks like it is probably from the cheaper end of the market.

I never will understand why people skimp on items such as this and yet spend more than they can afford on something less important, like a game console or state of the art television. Personally, I would rather have a decent kitchen first as, that way, I know I can cook everything with ease.

Still, each to their own I guess.

Bowl in hand I walked back down the hallway and through to the living room. My guest… Well, I say "my guest" but in truth, I suppose I am *his* guest. He is, after all, the home-owner here. The home-owner is standing on a chair. He has his hands tied behind his back and a noose around his neck. The other end of the noose is tied to one of the ceiling beams.

Ceiling beams!

You know you're in a posh neighbourhood when the houses have ceiling beams! It would have been rude of me not to acknowledge them by making use of them, right?

The man - I do not know his name - has tears running down his face as I sat down on his settee, close to where he was standing.

He is trying to say something to me but I gagged him before we started. I don't like it when they beg or scream. I find their words to be just "noise" and it gives me an almost instant headache.

I watched him for a while. He was moving his hands around, desperate to break free from the bindings, and yet standing very, very still. I can't say I blame him. If the chair topples, that is him finished with.

I set the popcorn down to the side of me on the settee. I could never do that in my own home. I have a dog who liked to jump up and sit with me and that little bitch, she sure does love popcorn. It is nice not to have to worry about her eating this. It means I can really focus my attention on the man.

'Ready?' I asked him.

He shook his head and tried to speak through the gag once again.

I shook my head. 'I can't understand you.'

With that, I kicked forward with my foot and knocked the chair from underneath him. He dropped down as far as the rope would permit and immediately started dancing around, suspended in the air. I laughed as I sat back in his seat and watched him dance his merry jig. He sure was going a funny colour in the face.

I put the bowl of popcorn in my lap and took out a handful. As I shovelled it into my open mouth, I realised just how much I had missed this. I sure do love popcorn.

HOBBIES

'Come in, come in…'

'Thank you. I'm sorry I am late.' Cathy added, 'Traffic was a nightmare.'

'It's not a problem. I'm just happy to see you again.' Paul closed the front door behind Cathy as she stepped in, out of the freezing rain.

It was eight o'clock in the evening. Cathy had been due at Paul's house half an hour ago but an accident on the road had caused an unexpected delay. To save Paul from stressing that she had stood him up - it was only their third date after all - she had sent him a text to warn him. True to form, he replied with a "thumb's up" emoji. Face to face he could hold conversation well and seemed like a genuinely interesting man, if not a little mysterious (which Cathy liked). In text messages though, he was always short and to the point. When they first started texting one another, Cathy worried he wasn't as keen on her as she was on him, given his messaging. It was only when they were next face to face, and she'd brought it up, did he explain he just wasn't very good at it. He said it felt "weird" to him to be chatty in texts when - if they waited - they could just have a good conversation in person.

'Can I take your coat?'

'Thank you,' Cathy said as she removed her soaked jacket. She handed it over to Paul who proceeded to hang it over the wooden bannisters.

'I've been meaning to install a peg or two,' he said.

Cathy laughed, 'I tend to use the back of my kitchen chair when I'm at home.' Unlike Paul, Cathy only had an apartment which she rented. No stairs so no bannisters for clothes to be flung over. Cathy breathed in and caught the scent of something cooking. She said, 'Something smells nice.'

'Should be ready soon,' Paul replied. He smiled at her and told her, 'You're in for a treat.'

'Well, if it tastes like it smells…'

Their first date had been a short affair; a trip to a coffee shop to see if they'd get on. Dates in coffee shops were easy. There was no pressure to stay for a whole meal if you didn't get on and you had all the time you wanted to make your introductions and do a little fact-hunting.

The second date had been a meal in Paul's favourite restaurant. He said it had been his favourite restaurant but - really - it had been the first time he'd ever gone there. Before he asked her out for the second date, he had Googled top restaurants in the area and that one had come up trumps. Sadly for him, given he was getting the bill, the price reflected its good reputation.

After the second date had been a success, and they had shared a few pleasant phone calls in the evenings which followed, Paul had invited Cathy round to his. From date one he had bragged about his cooking skills and had decided that - if she was into it - the third date would be the one in which he stood by his words. Cathy was only too happy to accept as she knew she liked him as a person but, until she'd seen where he lived, she wouldn't really *know* him. Where a person lives says a lot about the type of person they were, especially with the cleanliness of the abode.

'You have a nice home,' Cathy said.

Paul lived in a three-bedroom detached house in an okay part of the town. The house was nicely decorated, and everything seemed to have its place. It was clean too; almost impeccably clean.

'Thank you. I shall give you the guided tour later, if you would like. Although one room you might need...' He pointed down the end of the hallway and said, 'Lady's room is on the right.'

She smiled. 'Good to know.'

'Please, come through.' He walked ahead and led the way down the hallway and into the large kitchen. Dinner was cooking on the stove - a casserole of some description - and there was a nicely set-up table in the far corner. To add to the atmosphere, the room was lit with two candles on the table and a small light about the cooker so Paul could see what he was doing.

There was a bottle of wine chilling in an ice-bucket on the table, which Paul was quick to point out, 'I hope you notice the wine.'

Cathy smiled. 'I did.'

A red wine would have served better with a red-meat casserole, and would have been Paul's choice, but Cathy had stated she only ever drank white because red stained her teeth a blackish colour; not very sexy when you're trying to impress a date. Besides that, she found red wine tended to go straight to her head too.

'Cheapest bottle I could find,' Paul said. 'It actually felt wrong buying it.'

'Really?'

On their second date, Cathy had admitted to only really liking cheap bottles of white. If a wine was expensive, she found she wasn't keen on the flavour. If it was cheap, she said it had a kick to it which she found pleasant. Paul had just looked at her, stunned and confused. He was the opposite. The cheap bottles tasted like "piss" and the more expensive ones were heavenly. Some of them, at least. He did admit that there were some brands where you were only paying for the label.

'Well, if it makes you feel better,' Cathy said, 'I've bought that one before and I really like it.'

Paul smiled. 'That's the important thing.' He asked, 'Can I pour you a glass?' Without waiting for an answer, he walked over to the table and undid the screwcap of the bottle. Screw-cap. He preferred his bottles corked but, each to their own. Without digging at her for her tastes, he poured them both a tall glass before he set the bottle back in the ice-bucket. He didn't bother to replace the lid. Paul handed her a glass and then took his own up. He raised it and said, 'Cheers.'

Cathy clinked her glass against his and said, 'Cheers.' She smiled at him before she took a sip, excited about the electricity she was feeling between them. He smiled too but couldn't hide his disdain at the drink's obnoxious flavour.

'Holy crap, you really drink that?'

Cathy almost spat her drink back into the glass. She swallowed and laughed. That had been the first time he had said something in such a way. Usually he was so refined and particular with his words. She asked, 'You're not a fan then?'

'Honestly that is awful.' He asked, 'You really like that?'

'I do!'

'Well,' he smiled, 'that's the important thing.'

*

Just as it had done every other time they had talked, conversation flowed easily between Cathy and Paul. Over the dates they had discussed what they did for a living, they had discussed their dreams and aspirations. They had even had the awkward conversations as to how they can both still be single. Was it everyone else or were they both flawed in ways blind to themselves? The answer to the latter being that it was everyone else's fault.

'What about hobbies?' Cathy raised her glass and drained the last of the wine it held. Paul instinctively picked the bottle up and poured her another glass.

'Hobbies?'

'Yes, do you have any hobbies? Something to pass away the quiet evenings?'

'Erm. I guess I watch television.'

'That's not a hobby.'

'Surf the internet?'

'Not really a hobby.' To help Paul out, Cathy said, 'I like to play Badminton once a week. I like to paint too.'

'Paint?'

Cathy laughed. 'I'm not very good as I only started this year, but Bob Ross taught me a lot.'

'The guy with the hair?'

Cathy laughed again. 'The guy with the hair,' she confirmed.

'I don't think I have the patience. Also, it's not like it is a cheap hobby to start getting into, is it? You need paints, canvas… an easel, I guess.'

'True but, once you learn the basics, it is incredibly satisfying.'

Seeing the silver lining, Paul said, 'And I guess you could sell the artwork afterwards?'

Cathy laughed louder than before. 'Only if you know a blind person with a keen interest in collecting rubbish art.'

'I'm sure it isn't that bad.'

'I'll how to show you when you come over.'

Paul raised his eyebrows. 'Are you inviting me round?'

Embarrassed, Cathy hid her face behind her glass of wine ahead of taking another sip. 'Maybe.' She asked, 'Would you accept if I did?'

Paul laughed and took the opportunity to tease her, 'Maybe.'

'Oh "maybe" huh? It's like that, is it?'

'Well, you might not invite me yet. I mean the evening is still so young.' He added, 'We haven't even had dessert yet.'

Cathy changed the subject in a desire to know more about him, 'So are you really trying to tell me you have no hobbies?'

'When I was younger I used to collect butterflies.'

'Collect butterflies? You mean you would have them pinned to cards, all splayed out for display?'

'There was a little more to it than that but, in a nut-shell.'

'Oh, I'm not sure I would have liked that.'

'They're beautiful.'

'They are. But, to me, they're beautiful in the air, flying around.'

'True. But they never last long. My little hobby kept them beautiful for as long as I kept the collection.'

'You don't have it now?'

'No. Nowhere to really display them.'

'And you don't do it now?'

'I moved to the city. Don't really see as many butterflies in the city. Like bees, they're kind of sparse now.' He said, 'Just so you know though, when I was growing up, I never actually killed them. I would find them on the ground.'

'Really?'

'Really. I know some people caught them and killed them but, I never needed to.'

'Well, that's something. How do you feel about hunting?' Cathy was a big animal lover. It wasn't just butterflies she liked. One thing which would be a sure-fire deal breaker was if Paul liked to hunt, or even if he agreed with it.

'For sport? Is that what you mean? Because,' he explained, 'if it is hunting for survival then I'm all for that. We have to eat. If you hunt because you have to eat, or you need to make something from the skins… Then I don't have a problem with that, unless the animals are endangered in which case, I despise it. Hunting for fun though, just to show what a "man" you are, it's not something I agree with. In fact, I actually think less of a man who hunts. I don't think they're a "crack shot" or big and clever. I think they are pathetic. I think they are sub-human.'

'Sub-human? Wow.' Cathy couldn't help but laugh. She wasn't sure what reaction she was expecting from him, but it wasn't this.

Paul frowned and asked, 'Is this where you tell me that you enjoy hunting? Every Boxing Day you go out with your horse-riding friends and hunt down the foxes?'

'Ewwww no.' She added, 'And speaking of fox hunting, are those men and women even hunters? I mean surely they're just riding their horses. The dogs are doing the hunting and, for the most part, the killing.'

'I had a dream once in which a fox, on the back of a horse, was hunting down a group of men. They were using cats to help track them.'

Cathy laughed again. 'Really?'

'Yep. And I was sober when I went to bed.'

'Did you have cheese before you turned in for the night? Apparently that is good for giving weird dreams.'

'No. Cheese just tends to give me an upset stomach so that would have been an entirely different night.'

'Can't eat cheese? How do you live in life? Cheese is one of the finest pleasures... Give me a cheese board and some crackers and I am good for the day.'

Paul laughed. 'I didn't say I didn't eat it. I just know to expect a stomach ache with varying degrees of pain.'

'That sucks.'

Paul took a sip from his wine. He still wasn't used to the taste of the cheaper brand and - just as he had done with every other mouthful - he grimaced. He set the glass down and said, 'Okay so there is one hobby I have but it's a weird one.'

'Colour me intrigued.' Cathy asked, 'What is it?'

'Probably easier to show you.'

'Should I be concerned?'

Paul smiled. 'Maybe a little.'

'Well then, I guess you had better show me, huh?'

'Sure?'

'Yes.'

'Okay.' Paul set his glass down and stood. He extended his hand towards his date, to help her up from her seat. She took it and he gently pulled her to her feet. 'It's in the garage,' he told her.

Cathy said, 'I'm nervous.'

'You paint pictures?'

'Yes.'

'Well then,' Paul said, 'you like art.' He informed her, 'It's just art.'

'Okay well, like I said, I am certainly intrigued.'

*

Paul flicked the garage's light switch. The overhead bulb flickered a few times and - then - the lights came on. The garage was just as clean as the rest of the house. There was a work bench, with tools all neatly lined in a row for easy access. There was a large freezer. There was a car, covered with a special sheet to help protect it. There were a few pictures hanging. The pictures themselves seemed to be amateur in style and of various scenes - countryside, house interiors, warehouses - perhaps blown up from an iPhone, or something similar. Beside the pictures, there was a large metal cabinet from floor to ceiling and with several rows of drawers. Cathy's eyes were fixed on the pictures though. They were nice enough, sure, but not something she would have thought was good enough to be hung up. Especially given how expensive the frames looked.

'What's the story with the pictures?'

Paul almost seemed embarrassed that she had noticed them. He said, 'I took them with my phone. I know they're not very good but…' He simply said, 'Memories.'

'I like them,' she lied. 'Are they what you wanted me to see?'

'No. God no. I don't want anyone seeing those,' he said with a laugh. 'They're atrocious. I just like the memories they pull to the surface.' Paul pointed to the drawers. 'That's what I wanted you to see. Well,' he said, 'what's inside them.'

She looked at him with a puzzled expression. Paul made no effort to lead the way. He simply gestured towards the drawers with a wave of his hand. An invitation that, if she wanted, she could go and investigate them further. Curious about what was inside, she walked over and pulled the first of the drawers open. Inside there was a box frame. It was approximately 30x30.

'What's this?' Cathy didn't wait for Paul to answer. She lifted one out to get a closer look; a "look" she immediately wished she hadn't had. In a panic, she dropped the box frame to the floor with a scream and turned for the door.

She barely had time to register Paul's fist flying towards her face.

*

Cathy woke up from the blackness screaming. She was lying on a plastic sheet, still in the garage. Her legs were cold, her dress hitched up to her stomach and underwear pulled off.

'Nearly done,' Paul told her as he continued cutting away her labia with his favoured pair of sharp scissors. 'These will look mighty fine in the collection,' he said, almost drowned out entirely by her screams. Screams from the pain, screams from what was happening, screams from seeing the labia cut-away and pinned inside the box-frame as though nothing more than a delicate butterfly. 'Mighty fine indeed,' Paul repeated.

CAUGHT

'The first time I killed one, I stamped on her head and repeatedly punched it until her whole face caved in. I wanted to see if I could push her face so hard that it popped out the back of her head but, I never managed it much to my frustrations. I hid the body beneath my bed until I dare take it out to the garden where I buried it. I buried a few in the garden, including the second.

The second one was less violent than the first. I took her to the pond out back. I used the easy lie of wanting to show her the fish and she didn't kick up an objection. The moment we were there, I pointed to a fish that wasn't really there. I asked her if she could see it and she leaned down for a closer inspection. That was when I pushed her head under the water. I held her there until I was sure that she was dead and - knowing I was alone and would be for some time - I buried her close to the last.

To save accidentally digging in an already occupied spot, I used rocks to mark the graves. I didn't pile them up so that they were obvious, I just used a couple as placement-holders although - that wasn't their only purpose. I used rocks on the third.

I tied the third one up. I bound her ankles and I bound her wrists. She couldn't move as per my plan. I then took twenty steps away from her. For those who like a challenge, that might sound like a lot but, I'm fairly short so it's not really. In spot, I turned back to face her and then used my pre-collected rocks as ammo. I threw each one hard and fast and, to my delight, most connected. Each of the ones that did connect played their part in battering her body, cracking her here and there. By the time I had the one rock left, I walked to her still, damaged body and picked it up. I took it to the pre-dug hole and I dropped her into it. I used my feet and hands to push the dirt back over here and... That one rock which I left? That was the one I used for her placement.

For a while I didn't hurt anyone else. I kept myself to myself and invested my time in other hobbies. I did some writing, I played some games, I went for walks - I tried to do what "normal" people do. It wasn't long before I went back to my old ways though.

The fourth woman; I hit her in the mouth with a screwdriver over and over. Have you ever stabbed something hard down into someone's mouth to hear the crack of their teeth? Evidently it isn't as easy as it might sound, unless it was because she had a weird mouth but... I got frustrated and started bashing her against the brick wall. By the time I was done, she was lifeless. Despite that, I still stabbed into her a few times with the screwdriver. Each time it penetrated her body, I gave the handle a little twist to ensure her insides were nice and ripped up.

This was the woman I took to the garden only to notice there were other people there. My heart skipped a beat as I watched them from the shadows. They were gardening. Listening to their conversations, they seemed happy enough. They were milling around, doing their own thing and chatting amongst themselves so it was clear that - at that stage - they hadn't noticed anything unusual.

At that stage I didn't think about running away. My mind was fixed on the body I still had with me. The one I needed to dispose of. I got her away from the garden and kept her hidden until I could get her out to the woods. There, I tossed her into the shrubs. The thick undergrowth easily hid her from walkers - although, I had been sure to throw her far away from most of the dog-walking paths and cycle routes.'

'Right... So exactly how many of your sister's dolls and toys have you done this too?' Dad looked at me with a stern (and disappointed) expression on his face.

'You do realise she has been looking for some of those for a while now?' Mum chimed in. It was typical of them to gang up on me like this but, I was used to it now. They'd always preferred her over me. Sometimes I think they wished I had never been born.

'You know this isn't normal behaviour, don't you?'

I said nothing. I just sat on the edge of my bed. I could hear my sister crying from the other room. She had been crying since mum and dad took the toys back to her, after digging them up in the garden. Well, the toys they found. They haven't even got half of them yet.

'Are you even listening?'

I looked up at them and smiled.

THE
WHISPERING FORESTS

1

There is too much stress in life, don't you think? Even on days you have promised yourself not to check your work emails, not to answer calls or the door, not to think about work - something always comes along and blindsides you. It is frustrating and even though you can't help but think the world is against you, you need to keep in mind that you are just one person of how-ever-many billion inhabiting this god forsaken planet and, just as you're going through hell, so too are these people. Some will have it slightly easier than you but some will have it harder. Much harder.

Whatever happens in your life, whatever you are facing and no matter the severity of it all, it is important to remember to take a moment for yourself. I do it at least once a month. I pack a bag and I head out to the countryside. It is more than a few hours from my house, from my neighbours, my work, my normal life. It's not so far away it makes the journey impossible, and I urge other people to keep their "getaway" places within a realistic distance. Sure, it is nice to dream of faraway beaches with warm waters and golden yellow sands but all you're doing is torturing yourself. How often can you get out there? Once a year if you're very lucky. Some people will live their whole life without ever getting on a plane to such a destination. Do you think they dream of such destinations and then have their life end with disappointment? Or do they also set their goals realistically, like I do?

2

Most of the drive to my favourite spot is done on the motorways. If you time your journey correctly, you can work round most of the rush hour traffic. You might catch the tail-end of something but, it's never enough to really hold you up. Of course, there are occasions in which you might stumble across an accident but it is impossible to predict those. One blessing, though, is that most modern satellite navigation systems have minute-by-minute traffic reports so, if something does occur, they tend to give you plenty of warning with just a few beeps.

The drive is four hours, on a clear run. I tend to do two hours and then pull into a rest station. Once parked, I would typically find myself something to eat (usually fast food because I cannot stomach service station sandwiches) and then I'd walk around a bit in order to stretch my legs. Being stuck on the side of the motorway, there isn't usually much to take in but it's fine. I know where I am headed and know that the scenery there is something else entirely. In the service stations I tend to walk around the over-priced store and then just amble about the place whilst people-watching.

You see all sorts of characters in service stations. You see people from all walks of life. You see salespeople (usually with their phone plastered to the side of their head), you see families stopping off for some junk food as they head off (or home) from their vacations. You see couples. You see singletons. In fact - the only people you don't tend to see are homeless people but then, it is hardly surprising. It's not as though it is an easy place to get to, without a car or someone to give you a lift there.

One thing most people have in common in these places is that they all look tired and miserable. They know they're being ripped off with the prices they're being charged (even if they're only stopping for fuel). They know the food they're about to eat will be mostly shit. They know they still have a considerable journey ahead of them (if they didn't then they wouldn't have stopped). I try and smile at these people; something to brighten the day. Most don't see me. The ones who do, they just ignore me and carry on about their business. I don't say anything as there is little point. They don't know me so won't listen and, thankfully I never have to see them again.

I usually stop for about thirty minutes. I believe that is more than enough time to rest from driving. When I do get back in my car, I have confectionary from the garage and a coffee in the cup-holder.

When I'm back on the motorway, I put the car in cruise control and stick to the slow lane. Even on quieter runs people blast past me as they screech down the motorway in the fast lane (ignoring the fact the middle lane is empty). I see little point in driving like this. It's worse for the environment, it's worse for your petrol consumption and you're just asking to be pulled over and presented with a ticket. Slow and steady wins the race and - the whole point of going away is to get a break from stress. Driving slowly, through your choice, doesn't tend to lead to stressful situations. If you speed, you just wind yourself up when you eventually get caught behind someone who refuses to move. You hit the horn, you tail-gate, you swear at them and - for what? Take it easy. Go into the slow lane, put the radio on full volume and just enjoy the music. Or, like me, you could even sing along to it. It's not as though anyone can hear you. Enjoy yourself. It's one of the only times in your life where no one will be listening to you. Make the most of it.

3.

The first half of the drive there is the worst. It's only two hours but you feel every single minute of that time. The second half seems to go quicker. You know you're close. You know what is waiting for you. The excitement builds. You're on the home stretch. I don't make another pit-stop in that second half. There are public restrooms situated at the carpark spot I am headed for so, even if I start to need a piss, I know I can hold it. I have a few more years in me before *that* becomes a problem. At least I hope that is the case anyway, but you never know what the future holds.

My heart is practically bursting with joy when I do finally make the final turn into the carpark. It doesn't even bother me that there are other cars parked there and I struggle to find myself a spot. I know that, where I am going, it is well off the beaten track. There are no nearby cycle tracks, no paths for the dog-walkers, no routes for horses… You just have to push your way through the undergrowth and prickly shrubs and then, you're in your own private paradise. I smiled at the thought as I parked the car. I switched the car's tired engine off and leaned back it in the seat for a moment. Just a moment.

When I climbed out, I stretched my joints. Each one gave a satisfying crack, like the ones I would usually get first thing in the morning when I climbed from my bed. I grabbed my rucksack from the back seat, locked the car up and headed for the thicket which I'd have to fight my way through, but only when no one was looking. Why would I go through in secret? Because I don't want anyone thinking they're missing out on seeing something and trying to follow me. With my bag slung over my shoulder, and no toilet stop needed, I made sure the cost was clear and scrambled through the shrubs and bushes.

Some of the shrubs had sharp bits which stabbed into my exposed skin. It was more of an annoyance than particularly painful, but I promised myself I wouldn't let it darken my otherwise fairly light mood. What would be the point in letting that happen when I was so close to being where I had wanted to be?

I pushed on through to the other side and stumbled to the muddy ground. Thankfully the overhead canopies had protected the earth from much of the rainfall so, it was pretty dry. Mind you, had it been a little damp, it could have softened my fall a little. Still, nothing was broken (other than my pride maybe) and there was no one nearby to witness my fall. I picked myself up, dusted myself off and continued on my way. It would be about fifteen or twenty minutes before I got to my spot. After such a long drive, I welcomed the chance to stretch my legs and - as I made my way - I whistled a little tune of unknown origins.

4.

It had been a few months since I last had visited this spot and I almost missed finding it. One thing I hadn't counted on was how the trees and shrubs would continue to grow and change the area, almost to a point of being beyond recognition.

The view which I once cherished so, and the reason why I picked this area, was almost entirely obscured now by the overgrowing of trees. I made a mental note to myself that I should come back with some clippers, or something that I can use to cut away some of the branches. For now though, I simply pulled some of the branches back. Some bent back with ease, and those I wedged behind other branches to keep them in place. Others actually snapped off. The broken ones I dropped to the ground. I wasn't going mad and pulling them down all over the place. I was simply moving enough to make myself a window. A look-out point down into the valley below.

The view has changed over the months too. It is still breath-taking, which I am glad about. It just looks more "full" than before. More green, if that makes sense. But then, the last time I had been down here, it had been autumn time and most of the leaves had either fallen or turned brown in colour. I'm not sure whether I prefer the spring view or the autumnal one. I should take a photograph really, so that I can compare at a later date. Now though, I just closed my eyes and listened.

As I stood there, holding myself steady with a hand on the tree next to me, I took my precious moments to hear the world around me. Just like usual I could hear birds singing up in the trees. I could hear the running waters of a nearby stream. There was the sound of children yelling in the distance; no doubt playing games amongst the trees as they walk with parents close-by. If you pushed all of that from your mind though and concentrated harder, there was another sound too - the one that I had come all this way to hear.

The whispering.

5.

If you stood still, you could hear the sound of the wind weaving between the branches overhead. The movement caused the leaves to chatter, as they swayed in the breeze and most people would think that this was the sound I was referring to whenever I mentioned the whispering in the forests. That's not the noise I hear though. There is something else carried in the breeze. There are other voices.

There are four graves close to where I am standing. I know because I was the one who had dug them and I was the one who had filled them. I do not know the names of the people who reside beneath the dirt and - when I killed them - I am sure they did not know one another. But standing here now, listening, I am pleased to hear how they have taken the time to get to know one another.

I stand there and listen to them whispering to one another. They talk of the lives they lived, back before they met me. They talk of how we met one another, and they share secrets of what I did to them; leading them to be buried here. Some of the carried voices are mournful and full of self-pity and a couple of them seem entirely at peace;

like I had ended their suffering and sent them to a nicer place.

I can stand and listen to the voices all day. It's nice to know that - in the moments past our death - we are not entirely alone. We have the chance to meet other souls, the chance to communicate with them and - if the living concentrate hard enough - the chance to speak to those who still live.

I am glad that these souls found one another, and I am glad that, come the time of my death, I can reach out and find them once again.

THE VISITOR

'I did like you to start off with.' She smiled at him. 'I'm not sure if that makes you feel any better or not.' She sighed. 'It just wasn't working between us, and I am sure you'd agree. We were more like friends than lovers and,' she hesitated a moment before she continued, 'I just don't really need any more friends right now.'

Her name was Eleanor. His name was Mike. They'd met a few times, and, at the start, Eleanor had seemed invested in him but, it wasn't long before the cracks started to show. The first came when he passed wind in front of her and simply shrugged it off after saying it was better out than in. Then there was a chance of a date, after her plans changed for the night. He chose his friends and a pub crawl. So early into a potential relationship, if he was happy to see less of her and more of his friends then clearly, he wasn't as into her as she had hoped. It was several things and - here we are today.

Mike was strapped to her bed. She had got him into place using false pretences of a kinky time. The moment he was bound and trapped; she started her speech. It was a speech that eight other men had heard before him. Today his name was "Mike" but tomorrow, he would just be another ex.

'What are you talking about?' At that moment, Mike wasn't aware of his imminent danger. His prick was even still hard from where he was expecting it to be sucked ahead of being ridden. To him, it sounded like she was about to dump him but - if that was how she was feeling - why have him strip off and get on the bed like this? Why take the time to tie him down? Just tell him, he would leave, and she could get on with her night of whatever. 'So, what? You thinking we're better off just being friends with benefits?'

Eleanor frowned. 'Friends with benefits?' A moment later it sunk in for her. He wanted to be friends who just fucked each other. She shook her head. 'I'm not looking for a friend with additional benefits.'

Further confused, Mike asked, 'Okay I have no idea what you're trying to say then. You're saying you don't want to go out with me?'

'Yes.'

'But you made me remove my clothes and then tied me down, after asking if I wanted to have a little fun.' He looked down his bound body and asked, 'So what the fuck is all this then?'

Eleanor said again, 'I'm leaving you.'

'Right well… want to undo the fucking restraints so I can get my shit together and go then?' He shook his head. 'Fucking prick tease. This is seriously fucked up. You know that, right? Seriously fucked up,' he said again.

Eleanor waited for him to stop ranting and then calmly said, 'The problem with exes is that they have a nasty habit of popping back up when you are least expecting them. You could be out and about with a new partner, shopping maybe, and then - before you know it - you've bumped into an old flame in the supermarket. Then there is that awkward moment of just standing there, unsure of what to say. Do you introduce them to your new partner? Do you walk on and pretend you didn't see them? Do you stand and chat for a while, catching up out of politeness knowing full well that you're going to be getting grilled as soon as you leave the store? Who was that? How long did you date for? I've had it before; I was in a restaurant with a partner, and they seated us next to an old boyfriend. It's embarrassing and awkward and I don't like it. Which is why I do this…'

'Seriously, what in the actual fuck are you talking about? Can you just untie me so that I can go already? Fuck me. All you had to do was tell me on the phone that you didn't want to go out anymore and I wouldn't have bothered coming round. News flash, lady, you ain't all that into me either.'

'You're not really listening to me, are you?' Before Eleanor had a chance to explain herself, and her plans, more clearly there was a sudden knock at the front door. With a shocked expression she froze. Then, 'Who is that?'

'How in the fuck do I know?'

She frowned as there was another knock on the door. 'Wait there,' she said as she got up from the edge of the bed.

As she made her way to the bedroom door, Mike protested, 'You're not seriously going to go and answer that are you? Not with me in here like this... Just fucking undo...' It was too late. She had already stepped onto the landing and closed the door behind her, blocking out his words.

*

'I'm sorry for just swinging by like this but, can we talk?' Jack was standing on Eleanor's doorstep. He looked good; hair slicked back and wearing a suit. Eleanor wasn't sure if the suit was for her benefit or whether he had come straight from work. Either way, it was nice to see him even if now wasn't the most convenient of times.

'Now?'

Jack nodded. 'Unless you're busy?'

All Eleanor could think about was the man tied up on her bed upstairs and how thankful she was for not having put on a special outfit for him; a further way of enticing him to let her tie him up. As it was, she was still wearing her everyday clothes. The problem was, she *was* busy. She was busy getting rid of her past so that she could concentrate on the future she saw with Jack. She couldn't say that though for fear of pushing him away. *It was always the exes who got in the way of things.*

'No… Not at all,' she lied. 'Come in.' She held the door open thankful for the fact she lived in an older style house with thick brick walls and heavy doors. Sure, Mike would still be heard if he was shouting at the top of his voice but, he would at least be muffled. If Jack heard him, she would just say it was the television or something. Maybe tell him she was upstairs listening to an audiobook when he came knocking.

Jack stepped over the threshold and Eleanor closed the door behind him. She led the way through to the living room, aware that it was furthest away from Mike. When they were both in there, she closed that door behind them too.

'And just so you know, I don't tend to just show up unannounced.' Jack added, 'I just had to see you.'

In all honestly, it didn't impress Eleanor that he took the initiative to just show up. If he wanted to talk - good or bad - he could have called ahead first to make sure she was able to. Whilst it was, in part, sweet that he showed up like this - it also gave the impression that he thought of himself as more important out of the two of them. But then, before she jumped to any conclusions, she would hear him out. Once she knew what he wanted, then she would decide whether this was a bad move on his part, or something she was happy about.

'You said you wanted to talk,' she said. 'Should I be worried?' Usually, in her experience at least, when people said they wanted to talk it was never for any good reasons. First, they would ask to talk, setting expectations that something was serious, then they would say how they didn't think things were moving in the right direction. From that point on, the relationship would be over, and one would be left feeling guilty as the other wept having been blind-sided by the sudden declaration of lost love.

'No not at all,' Jack said quickly, stamping out any doubt she might have. But then, he started to doubt himself. 'Well, I hope it's not something you won't be happy to hear.' Jack took a deep breath in and said, 'I like you.'

'Well, that's good to know.'

'I like you a lot,' he said.

Eleanor smiled. His timing wasn't great but what he said was.

'I know we haven't been seeing each other for very long and how this is probably sounding to you but… I can't help it. You're all I think about. I wake up and you're in my thoughts. I go to bed, you're in my thoughts. Whenever I'm not running ragged at work, I'm thinking of you… And I know we're not exclusive yet…' He laughed and shook his head. 'I mean we've only been out a few times but…' He took in a deep breath and stated, 'I want us to be exclusive. I want you to think of me as your boyfriend. I want to think of you as my girlfriend. I want us to concentrate on each other and see where we go because, I'm not sure how you feel, I feel pretty good about us…'

Eleanor was just standing there, dumbfounded. She'd seen many men from the dating website. She had even gone on some dates with some women. Until now, none of them had been this upfront about their feelings. It was nice. Refreshing, even.

He was standing there. He had finished talking and was looking at her, hoping she would break the now-silence between the two of them. When she didn't, he continued, 'I mean it would be nice to hear what you're thinking.' He laughed nervously.

There was a slight pause before she said, 'I'm sorry I just wasn't expecting you tonight and all of this has taken me by surprise.' She continued, 'It's not every day someone says that to me…'

'Well, I would hope not even if I don't understand why. I think you're amazing…'

Eleanor felt her face flush from embarrassment. She couldn't help but to smile.

'Sorry. That was a bit much, wasn't it?'

'It's fine.' With thoughts of her guest upstairs so close to mind, Eleanor was struggling to think properly. She knew she couldn't give him an answer until she had sorted out her little problem upstairs. Quickly she said, 'I'm sorry but I was actually on the phone when you knocked. To my mum,' she was quick to add. 'I said I would call her right back. Are you able to wait here whilst I just pop upstairs and tell her I'll call her tomorrow?'

'Of course... Yes. I'm sorry, I really didn't mean to interrupt anything.'

'It's fine.' She walked towards the living room door and paused a moment before - without looking back - she said, 'So you know though... I think you're special too.'

Jack smiled. With the way she was acting, and her need to run off to call her mother back, he had been expecting the worst response. At least now he had hope that their conversation to come would be a good one.

She disappeared from the room, leaving him to his own devices.

*

Upstairs Mike was still struggling against his restraints but to no avail. They were heavy duty leather ones, complete with chains, purchased from a serious BDSM store. They weren't some cheap tat from a pauper's sex site. Cheap crap for those who didn't take the lifestyle seriously but knew they would be pulled upon as the bound person was tormented (albeit in ways by Eleanor not imagined by the people who were selling the product).

Eleanor walked in with a knife close to her body. Mike saw it. His mind didn't think anything worse than, 'What? You've lost the fucking keys? Oh, this just gets better and better. Well just be careful not to cut me with that thing, for fuck sake.' He added, 'Has anyone ever told you that you have issues? Like serious fucking issues.'

Eleanor said nothing. She simply walked up to the edge of the bed and then - coldly - ran the knife across Mike's throat. The shock in his eyes was instant as the blood started to pump from the gaping slit across his neck. Eleanor took a step back so as not to get any red on her. With this task done, she felt as though she could move on with Jack and not feel guilty that she still hadn't let someone else know they weren't for her. With this task done, she was one hundred percent single and okay to tell Jack that she liked him too and would be happy to call him "boyfriend". As for the mess left behind by this dumping; she could clean up later after Jack had gone home. The only thing she was unsure about was to whether the bedding would survive the fresh coating of blood that it was getting. This wasn't her usual way of disposing of her exes. Usually - with her preferred method - they would go home and die. Whoever found the bodies would be the ones who had to stress about the mess left behind. This was the first time she would have to be on clean-up duty.

Only when Mike stopped moving did Eleanor drop the knife down on top of his body. She stayed there a moment, staring down at him as he stared right back at her. Unlike her, he didn't blink though.

'Of all the days to change how I do things,' Eleanor muttered to herself, 'I get someone pop round for a chat. How's that for sod's law?' She sighed. 'I really wanted to take my time with you to show you my true disdain for you and how you treat women but... Had I known we were to be interrupted, I would have just stuck to my usual method.' She huffed. 'This had better not ruin things between me and Jack.' She paused a moment as she reflected on her own words. Then, she shook her head for a final time and headed back out of the room. She closed the door and continued back down to the living room where Jack was no longer waiting...

*

Eleanor stepped back into the downstairs hallway, from the empty living room. She could hear a noise coming from the kitchen. The sound of stirring. She frowned as she walked down to the kitchen. Jack was in there. He was standing at the kitchen work surface.

'What are you doing?'

'I thought you might not mind me making a cup of tea. I made you one too.'

Eleanor's heart skipped a beat. She noticed one of kitchen cupboards was opened and the black circular container - which was stored in said cupboard - was now by the kettle, with the lid off.

Jack pointed to the container and said, 'I wasn't sure how much sugar you wanted. I've a sweet tooth and - well - you probably don't want as much as I put in my own cup.' He laughed and took a sip. The smile faded from his face; replaced with a puzzled expression. 'That's odd...' He took another sip; a bigger gulp this time.

Eleanor said nothing. She was just standing there watching him with a panicked look. How was he to know that wasn't sugar? That what he had stirred into his hot drink was the very same poison she usually added to a date's drink when she was ready to break up with them? They would drink up, hardly aware. They would go home and go to sleep and - by morning - they would be dead.

'Milk might be on the turn,' Jack said. 'Good enough for now but might want to go out and get more tomorrow...' He took another sip.

THE BUBBLE

'We should probably wait for his social worker.'

'Why? He's already said he has done it.'

'I just think it would be better in the long run. He's clearly…'

'Playing the system.'

'Playing the system?'

'Playing us. Pretending he is as much of a victim as the actual victims. I've seen it all before.'

'When?'

'Really? You don't watch the news? You never read about serial killers when you were growing up? They all try and play the card.'

'The card? The "insanity" card?'

'Look at Sutcliffe. Sick son of a bitch killed all those women. He hammered them to death. He cut them up. He hid the bodies. Once he hid a body so well, he went back to move it so that it would be found. He was toying with the detectives. Yet when it came down to it, he plays the insanity card and spends most of his time in Broadmoor. An easier time served than what he would have faced in a real prison.'

'He ended up in a "real" prison.'

'Eventually. Most of his time was spent in Broadmoor though. You think the families of those he killed were happy about that? I can tell you, that would have been just another kick to their gut. They had their daughter, sister, child… They had their relative killed and the guy who did it gets an easy trip through the justice system. Fuck that. This prick in here has admitted what he has done. We have him. Yet you want to wait for his social worker to come in and drip-feed crap in his ear? Tell him that is it is okay because he isn't "well"? At the moment he isn't making any such noises himself, is he? He isn't blaming the system, society, his mental health. He's doing none of that bullshit.'

'I guess.'

'Like I said, we have him. So, let's get in there and finish it. Yeah?'

'Look I'll follow your lead, you know I will, I just don't want to do anything which might make the arrest illegal. He is admitting it, yes, but that doesn't mean his social workers and other healthcare professionals might not come down later and get the whole thing tossed out. I want to make sure it is water-tight.'

'God damn it. The guy has fucking admitted it. That's what is fucking me off. He's told us what he did. He has told us, coldly, the exact way he did it but… You're fucking right. They could still come down here and…'

Silence.

'I just think having him locked up in a nut house is better than the whole case being thrown out. Am I right?'

Silence.

'Fine. We'll wait. We always have the hope that another patient might do him over if he does end up in Broadmoor.'

'I'll pretend I didn't hear that.'

'Just makes me sick. Eye for an eye, and all that.'

*

'Okay for the benefit of the tape, accompanying Mr. Earls is his social-worker Mrs. Jackie Wilson. Mr. Earls has waived the right to a lawyer and has already been read his rights as per the previous recordings.

Mr. Earls, we know it has been a long night and you have already been through this and for that we apologise, but we are going to need you to take us through what happened one more time, please.'

'Sure. I don't have much money and I couldn't hold down a steady job. I was hungry. I was walking past the house and noticed the lights on and the front door wide open. The back of the car - on their driveway - was opened up and I could see a number of shopping bags in there.

From across the road, I watched as a woman came out of the house. She grabbed two more bags and then went back into the house. I only meant to run up to the car, grab a couple of bags and then get away again but - she came back out and she saw me. She screamed.

Before I knew what was happening, I pushed her back into her home and I hit her hard. She fell to the floor, hitting her head on the radiator in the process. That was when he - her husband I presumed - came out to see what was going on. I was panicking. I knew she was hurt bad, and I didn't want to go to prison so - before he had a chance to do anything - I lunged at him. We wrestled around and he got on top of me, pinning me to the floor. In that position I couldn't do much but scratch at his face. He yelled out in pain, but I didn't stop. Instead, I pushed my thumbs into his eye-sockets... I could feel my fingers push past his squidgy eyeballs and, I kept pushing as his screaming intensified.

By the time he went limp, I saw two children standing at the bottom of the stairs. They were just looking at me. Pale. Shaking. For a moment we stayed looking at one another, unsure as to who would blink first. When they went to move, so did I.

I beat them both because I knew, if I hadn't they would run and get help and I would - again - go to prison. I don't want to go to prison. I didn't want to kill them. Any of them. I just wanted to have some food. That was all. And that was what was going through my head as I was sitting there in the hallway, surrounded by the mess I had created. That was about when I heard the television playing from their living room. It was our Prime Minister and he sounded serious.

I walked into the living room and sure enough, Boris was doing an announcement. There was something about a virus. Corona, I think they called it although I can't remember. I'm not very good with names, you see. Anyway, it was serious and spreading through the country and world and people were dying. As a result, Boris was saying that we all had to stay in our homes now. We weren't allowed to go to work, we weren't allowed to see friends. We weren't allowed to do anything but stay home. They called it a lockdown.

Unsure as to what happened next, I remember grabbing the rest of the shopping from the back of the car and bringing it into the house. I closed the door and locked it with the top bolt. I just stood there with my mind going in all these different directions. I was thinking about what I had done. I was thinking about this plague. I was thinking how we were all now locked in and - here I was - in someone else's home. How many other people got locked in around someone else's home? I thought.

Although the situation was weird, I made the best of it that I could. I put the homeowners in the living room. I sat them up on the sofa and we would watch television together, we would play games together. I would tell them stories about my life and how I was struggling with all that was going on. Sometimes they would offer me advice; some of it was good, some of it seemed stupid. Just ways in which I could make my life better after lockdown came to an end.

We watched every broadcast the Prime Minister made to the people in the hope that things were getting better outside but, still, he kept us locked down. The only positive was that the family I was in a bubble with weren't eating much so, the food they'd purchased was lasting well.

When the lockdown did finally come to an end, I found it hard to say goodbye to my new friends. We had been through so much together and they had been so warm and welcoming, letting me stay in their home. I wished them well and said I would drop some money into them, next time I had some spare. My way of saying "thank you" to them. Although I still haven't managed to get anything dropped around to them because - well - things have been hard.'

'So, what did you do after you left them?'

'I tried to pick up my life. I went back to my old apartment. I threw out the bad food from the fridge. Things which had rotted whilst I was in lockdown with the other family. I tried to call my mum and dad to let them know I was okay, but they still refused to take my calls… I won't lie, it was hard. I was lonely.'

'So, when the second lockdown was put into place…'

'I went and found myself another family to stay with… I had such a lovely time the first time around that, it would have been rude not to…'

A MAN AND HIS DOG

7:00am - the alarm went off. He hit snooze and rolled back over. The dog, at the foot of the bed, did not stir.

7:15am - after the snooze alarm sounded, he got out of bed. His clothes were waiting nearby so he could easily slip into them. The dog didn't move until his owner headed towards the bedroom door. Then he got up too. Tail wagging.

7:25am - his teeth were brushed and remaining hair, of which there wasn't much, was combed neatly back. He looked into the mirror and remembered the younger version of himself and his full head of hair. He missed those days but still smiled at the tired face looking back at him.

7:30am - the dog tucked into his breakfast whilst he waited for the toaster to brown off his white bread.

7:50am - the morning walk. The walk took dog and man around the block. They walked side by side with frequent stops so that the dog could sniff here and there. The owner said nothing, not even to fellow dog-walkers despite the fact they greeted him.

8:30am - Walk complete. The dog had both urinated and passed stools. Depending on who was around, the owner may or may not have collected them up off the ground and put them in a trash. The dog was given a snack and he headed off to work.

12:01pm - He could come back from work. It was only a five minute walk from office to home so, no hardship. He greeted his dog and they enjoyed lunch together.

12:20pm - A quick walk with the dog. This was only ever around the block. The same route. An opportunity for the dog to stretch its legs and have a break too. Its owner took the time to bitch about the first half of his day; moaning about colleagues and customers alike if only to get it off his chest.

13:00 - Back to work and the dog climbed up on the settee for an afternoon nap. An old dog now, it had spent most days sleeping on the sofa in the afternoons and - as a result - the cushion had been permanently indented. The owner passed comment one day that he would replace the whole thing once the dog was gone. Until then, there was no point.

17:30 - He walked in after a depressing afternoon at work. More of the same old bullshit. Unpleasant customers, obnoxious colleagues who believed they were better than everyone else and the same static wages. Prices in the stores went up, utilities did the same and yet - always - he was overlooked for the wage increase. Why? Because he wasn't his manager's favourite staff member. He lacked the clearly necessary breasts. He was greeted by his old dog. Its tail wagging enthusiastically.

18:00 - The pair had dinner in the kitchen. He had fish with mash potatoes, along with some peas. The dog had its usual biscuits. Mixed in with the biscuits, there was some meat too to add to the flavour. The dog finished first and then watched over his master as he cleared his own plate. If the plate wasn't cleared, the leftovers were given to the dog.

18:45 - A nice evening's walk. Just the two of them. It's peaceful and gives him time to unwind from work and the dog another opportunity to go to the bathroom, which he always did. Other dog-walkers, or just "walkers", would be ignored and the quietest routes were always taken.

19:30 - the dog was given a bone to gnaw on. The owner kept his outdoor clothes on and told the dog he would be back a little after midnight. The dog looked up to him and smiled. Then, every day without fail, he said how many kills he wanted the owner to complete for the night. Furthermore, he told him which body parts he wanted brought back as proof. The owner smiled back and told him, as he did daily, that he would do his best. Then...

20:00 - the owner stepped out into the night, ready to drive around the town whilst looking for his latest victims.

SOMEONE'S HERE

I know someone is in the house. Everything was locked up tight, but I know, for sure, that someone is in the house.

I stalk through the house in darkness. There is a temptation to put a light on, but I know, in doing so, I would only be letting them know where I am. If they want me, they'll have to find me. Unless I find them first.

In my left hand I clutch my handgun with a strong grip. I've had partners, in the past, say they're entirely against handguns. I've lost relationships due to that but, I don't care. I'll never give up my right to a firearm. My right to protect myself.

The living room is still. Silent. No one around.

The hallway is still too, and it is here that I take pause. I listen to the house. Despite it being old, with unusually noisy pipes, it is quiet as a grave yet… I *know* someone is in here with me. Somewhere.

I don't call out, despite the urge. Again, I don't want them knowing where I am. I don't want to give them the opportunity to find me first. For all I know they have a gun too. For all I know, they're ready to aim it at me and pull the trigger the moment I show my face.

I'll be quiet.

I won't give them the upper hand.

I won't give them a free shot at me before I've had a shot at them.

The kitchen is empty of people.

There is a small office which is also empty. The computer is still on, despite the screen being off. The system is humming quietly away in the darkness and breaking the stillness. I won't lie, it's a small relief to have a noise. Still, I press on.

It's a small bungalow and there aren't many rooms left to investigate. Maybe I am being paranoid and - actually - I'm the only one here? Despite the thought, I don't let my guard slip. Not until I have checked every corner of every room. *Come out, come out wherever you are.*

The laundry room is empty too. Fresh washing hangs on a line and I catch myself breathing in deeply. Something about the smell of fresh laundry. Satisfied there is no one here, I go to check the last room.

I walk into the bedroom. There are two people here sleeping peacefully in their bed. I stand at the foot of the bed a moment and watch them. I can't help but to wonder what is going on in their dreams.

I'll never know.

I raise my gun and - in quick succession - I let off two shots. A bullet through the middle of their forehead for each of them.

I knew someone was in here. I bet there is someone next door too…

Enjoyed the stories? Check out Vimeo for some of Matt Shaw's short films!

https://vimeo.com/themattshaw

Want more Matt Shaw?
Sign up for his Patreon Page!

www.patreon.com/themattshaw

Signed goodies?
Head for his store!
www.mattshawpublications.co.uk

Made in the USA
Middletown, DE
13 October 2021